SAVING MEG

JAYNE DAVIS

D1714550

Verbena
Books

Manuscript development: Elizabeth Bailey

Copyediting & proofreading: Sue Davison

Cover Design: P Johnson

ACKNOWLEDGEMENTS

Thanks to my critique partners on Scribophile for comments and suggestions, particularly Jim, Lola, and Alex.

Thanks also to Beta readers Tina, Cilla, Dawn, Doris, Helen, Kristen, Leigh, Mary, Melissa, Patricia, Safina, Sarah, Sue, and Wendy.

orcestershire, December 1812
        Lieutenant Jonathan Lewis stopped by the fingerpost at the edge of the trees, the breath of his hired horse making white clouds in the frigid air. Although snow blanketed the landscape, drifting against hedges and plastering over the lettering on the sign, he knew his way. He was almost home—if Upper Westley could still be called that—and weary to his core.

The road to his left led to the village, not half a mile away. It was only mid-afternoon, but the tiny flakes of snow drifting down turned anything more than a few hundred yards distant into grey shadows, fading into the gloom.

Upper Westley was his destination today, but he hesitated. To his right, the dark gap between the trees marked the entrance to a narrow path through the woods, as familiar as the road. It was the short cut to Oakdene House that he'd used in his youth. Oakdene had been a refuge at times—a home where the man of the house had never been in his cups, and spoke only kind words to his family. Then, the wood had been a magical land in which he and Fred Rymer had fought imaginary dragons and rescued maidens from towers. One maiden, to be precise. Meg, Fred's freckle-faced younger sister, had acted the helpless damsel only under protest, climbing unaided in and out of the oak trees that were their castle turrets.

Jon shifted in his saddle, the creak of leather drowned by the sound of the horse snorting and pawing the ground. Meg was no longer a playmate—not to him, at least. That first leave, after he and Fred had been eighteen months in the army, had changed everything. Fred had been happy to tell tales of derring-do in the taproom of the village inn, but Jon had revelled in the peace and calm of Oakdene, and Meg's company. Meg had matured into an attractive young woman—very attractive indeed. Or perhaps he'd only just noticed that her hair wasn't merely brown, but the rich colour of chestnuts, and that she had a smile that went straight to his heart. His feelings then had gone far beyond friendship. He'd said nothing, for an impecunious soldier about to go back to war was no fit husband for any woman.

The mare tossed her head and took a couple of steps forward. He patted her neck and brought his mind back to his destination. Oakdene was less than a mile away through the trees, but the branches were too low for a man on horseback. It was at least a couple of miles by the lane that looped around the edge of the woods, and then it would be the same distance back before he could head down the road to the village inn and a room for the night.

Waiting another day would make no difference, surely? He should turn here and let the poor animal get into a warm stable; she'd worked hard today, carrying him all the way from Cheltenham, the snow deepening as they got further north. He needed rest himself, too—preferably a hot bath and a meal, then several days' sleep.

But he'd come here before visiting his mother because he'd promised Fred to take care of Meg and Mrs Rymer. It was over two months since he'd made that vow, kneeling beside his friend in the medical tent. And then repeated it to himself the next day as the chaplain read the funeral service over the hastily dug mass grave. Two months—but he could not have got here any sooner.

Squinting up at the sky, there were only swirling flakes against the grey. Tiny flakes at the moment, but who was to say what would happen overnight? The roads might be impassable in the morning. But the feeling was more than that. He wanted to call at Oakdene tonight, to see Meg, no matter how exhausted or travel-stained he was. Being with Meg would help him forget the first, and she wouldn't care about the second, nor would her mother.

He urged the mare on—she would get a warm stable, but not just yet.

Meg gripped the arms of her chair, resisting the impulse to pace the room. The cracking of the fire and the steady click of Mama's knitting needles only served to amplify her frustration. Everything appeared so peaceful—even the snow outside was only tiny, drifting flakes, floating gently downwards in the gathering dusk. Snow, isolating the house.

Isolating *her*—although that wasn't the snow, not

really. Despite Mama's presence, and the others downstairs, she had never felt so alone. Papa was gone, Fred was gone, and even Pamela and Sarah—girlhood friends from the village—had married and moved away. There was Jon—a true friend, and more—but she'd heard nothing from him since that one, brief letter from Burgos. Shouldn't he be back by now, if he was still alive?

No. *Be sensible, Meg!* Letters would return to England much faster than men, particularly men who might not be released by their commanding officers merely for the asking. But newspaper reports told of the British army being harried by the French all the way to the Portuguese border, and of this retreat being as harsh as the one to Coruña four years ago. Fred and Jon had survived that, and much else since. She *had* to believe Jon had survived this, too.

Someone knocked at the door, and Meg jumped up to open it, hoping she was not about to have another confrontation with Cousin Rupert. But it was only the cook, bearing a tray with tea and biscuits.

"I've brought you some tea, Miss Meg."

"Thank you, Mrs Baines." Meg stood back to allow her into the room. "I would have come down for it."

"It's no trouble, Miss. I was wondering if you're going to eat dinner downstairs today?" She set the teapot on the little table by the window. "Mr Rupert said he hoped you would."

"That would be nice, dear," Mama said, before Meg could answer.

"No, Mama," Meg said firmly, then turned back to Mrs Baines. "We'll eat up here. I don't want to make extra work for you, so I'll come down to fetch it."

Mrs Baines shrugged. "It's no trouble, like I said. It seems a shame, though, Mr Rupert eating alone every day. So helpful as he's been, ever since…" She pressed her lips together and finished setting out the cups and plates.

Meg sat at the table as the door closed behind the cook and rubbed a hand across her forehead. Worrying over this was bringing on a headache. Since Fred had died, this was *her* house, not Rupert's.

Rupert appeared to be so *reasonable*; that was part of the problem. His motives had only become plain—to her, if to no-one else—three weeks ago, and by then everyone around had come to the conclusion that he was a caring young man. After all, he'd put his own affairs to one side to help his widowed aunt and his cousin.

"Don't fret so, dear." Mama put her knitting to one side and came to sit by Meg, pouring tea for them both. "It will be all right soon, you'll see. He'll help you. He's a good man."

"Then why are we sitting up here instead—?" Meg stopped talking as Mama's face crumpled and tears glistened in her eyes.

"It's my fault, isn't it? Ever since my accident—"

"Never think that." Meg reached across the table and took her mother's hands. Mama had fallen down the stairs only a few days before they'd heard of Fred's death. The bang to her head had made her more easily upset, as well as affecting her memory. "I'm sorry for snapping at you. I'm only worried about what Rupert will do."

Mama pulled a handkerchief from her sleeve and dabbed her eyes. "I've said before, dear—it will be all right when he comes home."

"Fred won't be coming back." Meg gripped her mother's hands again. The words had come out more harshly than she'd intended. Her brother was dead, and no amount of wishing could change that. Sometimes Mama understood, but mostly she seemed to live in a world of her own, where everything would turn out right.

But Mama smiled. "Light another lamp, will you? It's time to shut out the night."

Meg sighed, and took a spill from the jar on the mantelpiece as Mama reached to close the curtains. She'd just lit one end in the fire when Mama spoke.

"There, I said he'd come."

Now Mama was seeing things! "Who has come?"

"Look, dear. I told you."

Meg cursed inwardly as she felt heat on her fingers, and threw the spill into the fire. She put her face close to the glass, rubbing to clear the mist from the cold panes. This window gave a view to one side of the house, and she made out the dark shape of a rider in the lane.

"It could be anyone." There were other houses further along the narrow road. "He will probably ride past."

Mama shook her head as she straightened and pulled the curtains together. "It was a soldier. I saw the shape of his shako. He said he'd look after us, and here he is. He wrote after he was killed, don't you remember?"

For a moment, Meg feared that Mama was talking of a ghost, but her sometimes addled wits had never taken her in that direction before. Not liking to display her forgetfulness about names, Mama had taken to never using names at all.

If she wasn't talking about Fred, who did she mean? Jon? He *had* promised to return as soon as he could. A tiny glimmer of hope started in Meg's chest as she peered out of the window again, but the rider had gone on.

Taking another spill, she lit the extra lamp with a hand that shook a little, and listened for the clop of hooves on the drive. A futile endeavour—the snow would muffle any such sound.

She opened the door and stepped onto the landing. From here she'd be able to hear what was said at the door —if Mama had been right. The feeling that someone might have come to help her—that *Jon* might be here— made her feel dizzy with relief.

As Jon approached the turning, Oakdene House became visible as a darker shadow in the gloom, a yellow glow showing from one of the upstairs windows. Then a hedge blocked his view until he reached the low stone gateposts that flanked the entrance to the drive. The snow was smooth here, unmarked by wheels or hooves. If it hadn't been for that glimpse of light, he might have thought the place deserted.

It felt wrong to ride this way alone, without Fred beside him. The last time had been almost exactly a year ago, both of them with a fortnight to spend in England while the battalion was in cantonments behind the Portuguese border. They'd arrived to find that Mr Rymer had died suddenly only the month before. A letter informing Fred of the fact had been awaiting them when they returned to the Peninsula.

The strength with which Meg had dealt with her father's illness and death while her mother grieved had drawn him towards her even more. But that had not been the time to declare himself, even if she had returned his regard. Instead, he'd kept in the background during those two short weeks, running errands when asked, removing himself from the family's grief when there was nothing for him to do. He'd grieved himself—Mr Rymer had been a better father to him than his own.

Now here he was again, in depressingly similar circumstances.

A glimmer of light showed through a gap between the curtains in the parlour as Jon dismounted and looped the reins over the mare's neck. He plied the knocker and stood back, waiting impatiently until he heard footsteps in the passageway.

The Rymers' manservant opened the door, wearing an apron over homespun breeches and waistcoat. He regarded Jon with round eyes, before a smile spread across his lined face.

"Mr Jon!"

He stood back, opening the door further, and Jon stepped over the threshold. "Farlow—good to see you. Is Miss Rymer at home?"

Before Farlow could answer, another voice spoke. "Miss Rymer is not receiving guests." A man came out of the parlour, clad in a well-fitting blue tailcoat over grey waistcoat and pale trousers. Jon was trying to place him when a sudden scuffle at the top of the stairs drew his attention. He thought he saw a swirl of a black skirt through the bannisters, but no-one came down.

"My cousin is indisposed," the newcomer said. "Farlow, you may return to your duties."

Cousin? Jon racked his brain as the manservant

grimaced behind the newcomer's back and vanished through the kitchen door.

Rupert… Rupert Taylor; that was it. A connection on Mrs Rymer's side of the family.

"Mr Taylor." Jon nodded briefly.

"And you are…?" Taylor ran his eyes down Jon's greatcoat to his boots, both dripping into a spreading puddle on the floor. His eyes narrowed. "Lewis, isn't it? The drunken farmer's son? Margaret won't want to see you. Her brother would still be with us if you hadn't encouraged him to join the army."

What?

Taylor came closer, too close. Jon took a step back, into the flakes of snow beginning to drift in through the open door.

"Besides, she has other things to think about now, rather than reliving the past. A new future to look forward to." He smiled. "We are betrothed. On Tuesday, Miss Rymer will become Mrs Taylor."

CHAPTER 2

Meg's happiness at hearing Jon's voice turned to fright as a bony hand covered her mouth and another gripped her arm. Her nostrils filled with the smell of stale tobacco that always hung around Morrison, Rupert's manservant.

Heart racing, she twisted her head from side to side as he dragged her along the landing, but her struggles had no effect. She pulled against him again, but he didn't let go, his strength surprising for such a thin man. He did, though, stop moving—standing still enough for her to hear what was being said at the front door.

"...still be with us... reliving the past... betrothed... Tuesday..."

No! Meg turned her head and bit Morrison's hand, but although he muttered a curse, his grip on her only tightened. She kicked out—anything to let Jon know she was here—but Morrison grabbed her around the waist with his other arm and lifted her so her feet flailed above the floor.

And then it was too late. Jon's voice came, the words all too clear. "I wish you both well, Mr Taylor. Please give my regards to your cousin and aunt." And the door closed with a thump.

Jon mustn't leave without talking to her! Such a close friend surely wouldn't believe she wanted to marry Rupert?

She slumped in Morrison's grip. Why wouldn't he believe it? Everyone else did.

The rasp of bolts being shot home on the front door spurred her into another struggle. If she could get to a window and call…?

This time Morrison let her go, rubbing his bitten hand. Meg raced along the landing—her room looked over the drive.

Her hand was on the latch when hard fingers closed around her arm again. Morrison—and Rupert stood behind him.

"Tell your man to take his hands off me," she spat.

Rupert nodded, and Morrison let go. Rupert jerked his head, and with a poisonous look at Meg, Morrison clattered down the stairs.

"Is something wrong, dear?" Mama asked, coming out onto the landing. "Has he gone away?"

"All is well, Aunt Mary." Rupert's voice oozed reassurance and sincerity—the tone that had fooled Meg, too, at first. "It was only someone asking directions. Why don't you rest before dinner?"

Mama smiled as he led the way back to the bedroom and ushered her in.

"No need to upset your Mama," he said, coming back to Meg. "We wouldn't want to have to bring Mr Busby back, would we? You know he wishes to treat her in his sanatorium."

Meg turned and stalked down the stairs and into the parlour. She rounded on Rupert as he entered behind her. "Are you proud of yourself? Threatening women—blackmailing—to get your own way? And allowing your man to *assault* me?"

"Needs must, my dear." He sat in a chair by the fire and picked up a glass of wine. "And it's hardly a threat to wish for my father's sister to get the best medical treatment for her condition."

Meg's fingernails dug into her palms as she restrained the impulse to shout at him. Or throw things. They'd already had this argument several times. It was not even an argument, really—he just kept saying the same thing in a calm tone as if explaining something to a simpleton. So calm that, if any of the servants had been listening, they would have praised him for keeping his temper when faced with an unreasonable and hysterical woman.

"Have some wine, my dear Margaret. It might help to settle you." He held a glass out, but she ignored it. "I do begin to wonder if your mother's accident merely triggered some... some inherent weakness in her brain. It is to be hoped that such a weakness is not hereditary."

Meg stared at him and shook her head. Was he threatening her now? But she mustn't argue—that would only please him, and if the servants heard her raised voice, it would support his case.

"Why did you send... Lieutenant Lewis away?" It might be wise not to reveal how close their friendship was. Or had been. She pushed that thought aside.

"What good would it do you, or Aunt Mary, to hear

the details of poor Fred's death? Aunt Mary is… fragile enough."

"I see." She took a deep breath. "How considerate of you, cousin."

"I trust you are not stupid enough to attempt to send a message to him?" He was examining his wine, as if this conversation were of minor importance. "The servants know on which side their bread is buttered."

They did. It wasn't that they were disloyal; more that Rupert had convinced Mrs Baines and Annie that he would be a good master to work for, and that Meg was being missish in her reluctance to marry him. And Farlow —she'd thought to send him with a message to the vicar, but he'd had no reason to go into the village since Rupert had come. No doubt everyone would say how helpful Rupert had been, seeing to all the ordering of food and paying of bills.

Meg shrugged. "How would a message to the Lieutenant help me? Besides, it is still snowing—I doubt Farlow could reach the village in this weather." That wasn't a terribly good reason—Jon had reached Oakdene, and not ten minutes ago. "You've never been here in winter, cousin, but the road to Upper Westley is notorious for getting blocked when it snows." That would be news to the villagers, but Rupert was unlikely to detect her lie.

"Good. I'm glad to see you're being sensible, Margaret." He waved a hand in dismissal and picked up a book. Seething, Meg bit down on her anger and controlled the impulse to slam the parlour door behind her.

It was Sunday—the banns would have been read for

the third time this morning. Rupert had prevented her from going to the village these last few weeks, so she'd had no chance to talk to the vicar, or anyone else who might help her.

Her only option was what it had always been—to deny she was willing to wed when they got to the church. But she had a lowering feeling that it would merely delay the inevitable. Rupert would still pressure her to accept, and might well have the sympathy of everyone else. After all, only a hysterical woman would change her mind like that at the last moment.

It was Rupert's threat to Mama that worried her most. He could still send Mama to an asylum if she married him, of course, but she suspected he would not. That would use up some of the money he would gain from becoming the new owner of this house and the farms.

No!

Jon stepped back from the door as it shut in his face, his hands clenched into fists.

It could not be true. Could it?

He stared at the door as if it might answer him, then looked up. Above, the windows were dark—no-one was trying to call him back, saying there had been a mistake.

Swallowing against rising nausea, he took a deep breath and hunched his collar higher. Meg—the Meg he used to know—would have welcomed him in, sent Farlow to stable the horse, and produced a hot toddy and a meal. She would have done so even if she were betrothed to another man. They were still friends, and she knew Fred had persuaded him to join the army, not the other way around.

Did females find Rupert Taylor attractive in a way that he couldn't see? Certainly he was better dressed than Jon, whose greatcoat and faded red jacket bore the signs of the hard retreat across Spain and his travels since. But there had been something odd in Taylor's expression—a gloating, self-satisfied look. Then there had been that movement at the top of the stairs. Had Taylor *prevented* Meg from seeing him? Did Meg really want to marry the man?

He would come back later to find out.

Feeling a little better with that decision made, Jon led the mare on around the house and past the small building where the Rymers kept their horse and gig. He turned beyond the hedge that separated the gardens from the surrounding fields and headed for the woods. He would return on foot later—he needed to speak to Meg without anyone else seeing him, and the horse would give him away. If he led the animal through the trees now, they would make a trail that would be easy to follow when he came back in the dark.

The white swan on the inn sign was invisible through its coating of snow, but welcoming light spilled out of the windows. Jon rode down the lane at the side of the building and dismounted in the small stable yard.

"Anyone there?"

He had to shout again before a door opened and a figure shuffled out, a sack keeping the snow from his head and shoulders.

Jon recognised the man's limp. "Harding—how are you?"

The figure straightened and squinted into his face. "Lewis? Bloody hell, man, what happened to you? You don't look at all well." He took the mare's reins and led her into the stables. "Come far?"

"Only from Cheltenham today." And all the way across Spain and Portugal before that, then the packet boat from Lisbon to Falmouth. The journey had seemed longer and harder because Fred wasn't with him.

"Bad business, Captain Rymer getting—" Harding broke off. "Get yourself inside. I'll hear all about it later, no doubt. No, go in the back way; it's nearer."

Jon did as he was told, slinging his saddle bags over his shoulder and pushing open the rear door into the scullery. Opening the kitchen door, a wall of warm air hit his chilled flesh, thick with the rich smell of fried onions and roasting meat.

"Jonny Lewis!" The landlady turned from the kitchen table to look him up and down. "Sam! Look who's arrived!"

Jon winced at her shout—Mrs Munnings was used to making herself heard above the babel of a busy taproom, but even his sergeant would have been proud of such a voice.

"Are you wanting a room? Of course you are. You look proper frozen, and half-starved as well. Get yourself into the taproom—I'll send some soup through while I sort out a bath and a room."

He'd had some idea of asking what she knew about Taylor, but her plan sounded exactly what he needed. A warm body and full stomach first, then information.

CHAPTER 3

*H*alf an hour later—thawed, clean, and shaved —Jon sat in the inn's parlour with a plate before him full of thick slices of beef and rich gravy, accompanied by roast potatoes and parsnips. He still wore his stained trousers, hastily dried in front of the fire, but Mr Munnings had lent him a clean shirt while one of the maids laundered his own linens. Apart from worrying about Meg, the only things stopping him from fully appreciating his dinner were his bone-weariness and the numerous pairs of eyes watching him.

Watching and waiting—at Mrs Munnings' insistence— before interrogating him about Spain and Portugal and what had happened to poor Fred Rymer. Things he didn't want to talk about, not yet. Fred's death, and the losses his battalion had taken on the long trek across Spain, were still too recent, too raw.

"Tell me what's happened here while I've been away," he said, to break the unnerving silence. He let the talk wash over him—someone's wife had run off, someone else had opened a new shop, the farm where Jon had grown up had been sold again…

It wasn't until someone mentioned Captain Rymer's name that he started to pay attention.

"Seems they're all set up." That was the clerk Mr Trythall had taken on when Jon decided that learning to be an attorney wasn't for him. "Miss Rymer's marrying that Taylor chap."

"Cousin, isn't he?" someone else said. "Good of him to come and help out when Mrs Rymer fell."

"…never been the same since…"

"…can't remember much, they say…"

Meg's mother was ill?

"Needs a man about the house, if you ask me."

Not Rupert, Jon thought savagely.

"Nice chap. Was ever so friendly when he came to get his horse re-shod. Said things have suffered there since Mr Rymer died…"

"…so sad…"

"…Taylor paid their bill for them…"

"…hard for two women to manage alone…"

"…bought extra sugar and tea—said they needed cheering up…"

"…woman has no business dealing with rents and leases…"

"Give the poor man some peace," the barmaid said, distributing another round of ale as the audience nodded and shrugged. "In fact, take yourselves off to the taproom and let him finish his meal."

Jon gave her a grateful smile. Becky had been doing this job since he could remember, and seemed to know everyone's business, but she always had a kind word. Amid good-natured grumbles, the others allowed her to usher them out. A few minutes later she returned with a dish of steaming apple pudding and a jug of cream, moved his empty plate to a nearby table and sat down opposite him.

"Did you call on your mother on the way, Jon?"

"Not this time. I came here first, straight from Falmouth. I promised Fred I'd look after his family. I'll visit Mother on my way back." He picked up the spoon she'd set beside the bowl, but didn't eat. "What happened to Mrs Rymer?" Poor Meg, having to deal with that as well as Fred's death.

"Fell down the stairs, she did, and banged her head. Never been quite right up here since." She tapped her temple. "That wasn't much before we heard about Captain Rymer. Good thing she'll have someone to help her with everything."

"I heard," Jon said, trying not to snap the words. Was he the only one who hadn't taken to Taylor? "From Taylor himself, before he shut the door in my face."

Becky's brows rose. "That don't sound nice. He was a pleasant enough bloke when he come in here. Come to look after them, he said, when Mrs Rymer didn't get better. But shutting the door in your face, and you come all this way…" She shook her head. "Funny thing, though —I don't remember seeing Miss Rymer in the village since the banns was called."

"Perhaps she's busy looking after her mother." For Meg's sake, he hoped that was the only reason.

Becky frowned, then went over to the door. "Charlie Allsup!" Her voice could rival Mrs Munnings'.

Allsup? The grocer? A couple of minutes later Charlie came in—a youth of sixteen or so.

"What did I hear you saying about delivering to the Rymers last week?" Becky asked, resuming her place opposite Jon.

"Last week?"

"You was complaining about cake."

His face cleared. "Oh, yes. I delivered their order last week, and that Taylor told me to leave the stuff and clear off, didn't even give me the time of day. No chance to get a word in edgeways, never mind the bit of cake their cook usually gives me."

Something was definitely wrong there.

"D'you think Miss Rymer wants to marry him?" Becky asked, once Charlie had left the parlour.

"That's what I want to know," Jon said. "I'm going back to find out later."

Becky gave a nod of approval. "You look dead to the world. Have you had enough to eat?"

"Enough for now, thank you." In truth, he wanted nothing more than to lie down somewhere. A full stomach, a pint of ale, and the warm room were conspiring with his fatigue to put him to sleep.

"Go to bed." Becky stood. "I'll come and wake you at… What time?"

"Eleven." If he set off then, everyone in the house should be asleep by the time he got there—including Meg, quite possibly. But if he went earlier and Taylor was still up, he would just be shown the door again. He knew which was Meg's window, and it wouldn't be the first time he'd thrown stones to wake someone.

Five hours. He felt as if only a full week in bed would ease him, but five hours would be a start.

"Don't forget, Becky, will you? No helpful ideas about me needing more rest!"

"I'll get you up, don't worry."

Meg lay awake in her bed, as she had done often in recent weeks. She'd eaten dinner with Mama in her room rather than have to sit with Rupert. Mama had retired to bed, sure that everything would be all right now Jon was back. Meg had expressed agreement and retreated to her own room. If only Mama could be right this time.

Downstairs, the clock in the hall chimed the half-hour. Or was it one o'clock? She'd heard the thing tolling midnight what seemed like hours ago.

Did Jon's return change anything? She felt as if it should, but if he'd taken Rupert's words at face value…

No—he could not have done. She turned onto her back, staring up into the darkness. Outside, everything was eerily still, only the wavering call of an owl breaking the silence. A thin sliver of moonlight coming through the curtains indicated that the clouds had cleared.

Another hoot. She loved the sound of tawny owls—so much more tuneful than the screech owls that normally called from the woods.

Owls? When Jon used to come to get Fred for a midnight adventure…

Meg flung back the covers, pulling a wrapper on as she crossed to the window and drew one curtain back. The world outside was patterned in black and white, moon-

21

light bright on the snow and the shadows inky. Nothing moved.

There! As the owl sounded again, a figure stepped out of the shadow of a hedge.

Jon *had* come back!

Heart racing, she opened the window and waved, shivering as the chill air tumbled into the room. Jon raised a hand and pointed sideways, towards the small stable, then disappeared back into the blackness.

Clothes—never mind stays and chemise. The moon lit enough of the room for her to find the gown she'd worn earlier, and she dragged it on over her night rail. Easing open a drawer in the chest, she found her thickest pair of woollen stockings and pulled them on. That would have to do.

The landing outside her door was black, but moonlight lit the stairs. Meg crept along quietly, memories from her youth telling her which squeaky boards to avoid. She got down the stairs without a sound, and went into the kitchen.

A shape huddled in a chair by the stove spoke quietly. "Evening, Miss."

Meg thought her heart had stopped. She let out a shuddering breath as she realised it was Farlow, not Rupert's man. He opened the stove door and pushed something in, then stuck the lit candle into its holder and set it on the table.

"Why are you here, Farlow?"

"Not my choice, Miss. Mr Taylor said someone had to be awake to make sure 'that Lewis man' didn't try to get in. They were his words."

"Oh." Had Rupert told Farlow to stop her going out?

"I… I was going to the stable to see if the cat's had her kittens yet." That was a stupid excuse. Farlow knew as well as she did that the cat wasn't expecting.

But Farlow nodded. "You'd be worried about her, yes." His lips curved. "If Mr Taylor or that bean pole that calls himself a valet find you went out there, neither of them would know whether the cat's about to have a litter. And they never told me to stop you going to the stable."

Meg closed her eyes for a moment and let out a breath of relief. "Farlow, why…?" Why was he helping her now when he'd seemed to approve of Rupert's presence?

"He fooled me, I'm afraid to say, Miss. Thought he meant well. But Annie was setting the fire in his room yesterday when Mr Jon called. She saw what Morrison did, and not a word of reprimand from Mr Taylor." He shook his head. "And I remember Mr Jon—he was a good lad. I remember the owls, too, and Mr Fred creeping out."

"Thank you, Farlow." If only he'd understood Rupert's true nature earlier—but that was irrelevant now. She pushed her feet into her old boots and, with a glance at Farlow for permission, took his thick coat off its hook and thrust her arms into the sleeves.

The latch on the back door made little noise, and she picked her way carefully across the moonlit yard. Farlow had cleared the snow in the afternoon, but the thin layer that had fallen since then had frozen into a treacherous sheet.

Jon let himself into the stable with relief, pleased that he didn't have to start digging in the snow to find stones to throw at Meg's window. He left the door open a little so he could see the kitchen door. He wasn't sure what he would do if Meg didn't come, but he should give her some time before starting to worry about that. He tucked his hands beneath his armpits in an attempt to thaw his fingers. At least in here, the horses provided a little warmth, and he was sheltered from the icy breeze. The animals shuffled in their stalls, dim shapes in the feeble light filtering through the windows. The dappled grey was Daisy, the Rymers' old mare; the other must belong to Taylor.

Finally, a dark shape picked its way across the yard, moonlight removing any colour. Meg. He pushed the door open further, then pulled it closed behind her.

"Jon?" Her voice wobbled. "Oh, Jon!"

Without thought, he reached out and drew her towards him, holding her close. She rested her head on his shoulder, her body shaking.

"Meg?"

"I'm sorry." She lifted her head and sniffed, but her voice sounded no steadier than before.

"Don't be." He raised a hand to her head, pressing it gently against his shoulder again. "Have a good cry, then tell me." Leaning his cheek against her hair as he wrapped his arms around her, he breathed a faint scent of rosewater. Suddenly he didn't feel cold at all. He'd wanted this since that leave after Coruña—but not in these circumstances.

CHAPTER 4

*J*on cursed Fred in his mind as he felt Meg's body gradually relax against his own. It wasn't as if Wellington were short of officers —there would have been plenty of others happy to buy his commission if he'd sold out last winter and come home to take his father's place. But Fred had always hankered after an army life, and had no desire to spend his time doing nothing more than overseeing a couple of tenant farms.

"Jon, I'm so happy to see you," she said at last, lifting her head from his shoulder.

He hugged her a little tighter. "It's good to see you, too." Better than good—as if he were home, and they belonged together.

About to ask if she really was going to marry her cousin, he thought better of it. She'd never clung to him like this before. Even if her trouble wasn't Taylor, she'd no business marrying a man she couldn't go to for comfort.

"Tell me about it, Meg." He looked around, straining to see in the gloom. There—a bench against the far wall, beneath pegs holding bridles and reins. "Come, sit down. I've a feeling it will be a long story."

"Not that long."

But she allowed him to lead her to the bench and they sat, shoulders and thighs pressed together. Was it wrong to regret the too-many layers of cloth between them?

"Rupert wants me to marry him."

"And you do not wish to." He needed to hear it.

"No."

Good. A little of the tension in him relaxed. "You could just tell him that." He made the suggestion tentatively— the Meg he knew would have no hesitation in doing so, and he did not wish to sound critical.

"I have, but he takes no notice. He says I'm being hysterical. He says the worry about Mama's fall and then Fred's death is affecting my mind, and he's only doing what's best for me and I should be happy about it."

"Fred did describe him as a lying weasel." He hadn't seen Taylor often when they were all boys, but he did remember Fred's antipathy.

"But I'm not afraid of weasels." Her voice was quiet, defeated.

Afraid of Taylor? He must have some hold over her for this situation to have arisen. Jon took a deep breath, suppressing the wish to break into the house and drag Taylor outside, to make *him* afraid. "I didn't mean to make light of things, Meg. Tell me from the beginning."

"When the letters came…" She stopped and shook her head. "No, not long before we heard about Fred, Mama tripped on the stairs. She seemed to recover, but she's… she's forgetful now. She can remember some things—like how to knit and sew—but not names. And sometimes she forgets things that happened in the past."

So Meg had had to deal with the news of Fred's death without her mother's support. "And Taylor?" he prompted, when she did not continue.

"I wrote to my uncle to let him know about Fred, and Rupert came here straight away. He took a room at the Swan, that time. I thought it was good of him to come to see if he could help. Everyone else did, too—even the vicar said what a helpful young man he was."

Wanting to hear Fred's will, more like, Jon thought savagely.

"He asked me to marry him. He sounded really kind, as if he did want to support me."

How else could he get his hands on the Rymer farms? The ones Meg had been dealing with perfectly well for a year, since the death of her father.

"I said no, and he went away—he seemed to accept my decision. But he came back a few weeks later. Mama... By then, Mama was up and about, but she was still forgetful, or doing silly things like putting salt in the sugar bowl. She gets upset more easily than before, too."

That might not be the result of the accident—Mrs Rymer had lost a husband and a son in a year. And Meg had lost a father and a brother. It wasn't surprising she didn't feel she could cope with her cousin's machinations.

"What did Doctor Curtis say?" He remembered the local doctor as a sensible man.

"There's nothing he can do. She manages perfectly well, mostly. He said time should help, and to try not to worry her. But Rupert... Rupert said a country physician wasn't good enough, and he paid for a man to come from

London. He wants… Oh, Jon, he says he can cure her if she goes to his asylum. Mr Busby said that patients' minds become lazy, and have to be shocked into remembering. Rupert described the treatments—ice cold baths and a low diet. And he talked about keeping them calm by not allowing them to see their families until their memories came back."

"Sounds more like torture to me," Jon said, and regretted his words as Meg gave a little gulp. "Rupert thinks this is a way to *help* your mother?"

"He says so, yes. Sometimes I wonder if he's right, and I am harming Mama by not allowing this doctor to…" There were tears in her voice again.

With a muttered curse, Jon put his arm around her and hugged her close. "Never think that, Meg. Is your mother happy—can you tell?"

"I think so."

"Well, then."

"He says his father is Mama's brother, and has a right to ensure she has the best treatment."

Marriage wouldn't change that. "Let me guess, Meg. He says your Mama will be calmer with a man around the house, and if you will only marry him it might not be necessary for her to go to this asylum."

He felt a movement as she nodded. "Something like that, yes. But he could still send her away if we marry. The vicar called the banns without asking if I wanted the match."

The sudden change of subject threw him for a moment. "Did you not object when you heard them?"

"Rupert tried to stop me from finding out. It was a sunny morning, and Mama had a headache, so I walked through the woods to go to the service instead of taking the gig. I tried to stay behind afterwards to tell the vicar I didn't consent, but Rupert had arrived by then and took me away. He said Mama was ill and I was unwise to have left her alone."

"She wasn't ill," he guessed.

"No, she wasn't. But the vicar must have thought I wasn't looking after Mama properly. And Rupert has stopped me going into the village since then."

"You only have to say no in the church, Meg."

"I know. You must think I'm a weak fool."

"No, never that." Not when she'd had so much responsibility thrust upon her.

"I… I feel so alone, Jon. I know Rupert cannot make me say yes, but then I remember that the vicar read the banns without my permission. And Rupert… he's been talking to the magistrate. Farlow drove him there in the gig, and said he looked pleased when he came out. He is always saying things like a woman cannot manage the farms, and I worry that he's right. Or even if he's not, that everyone else will think so and they'll wear me down, and it will cause a huge fuss if I say no in the church…"

"Hush, now. A fuss doesn't matter, and you're not alone while I'm here." He'd start by talking to Mr Trythall tomorrow—the attorney had been a good friend to him in the past. "You have friends in the village." Becky, at least, and probably Mrs Munnings, too, once Becky had told her the situation. Not that two women would have much influence against the magistrate or the vicar, if the men took Taylor's side. No-one could *force* Meg, but he could see how continual pressure might wear her down.

"Mr Trythall will help you."

"But you'll go back to Spain, then I'll be alone again. And you might not come back this—"

"Don't worry, Meg. I'll make sure Rupert takes himself off—permanently—before I leave. Besides, the battalion's being sent to Jersey—not nearly as far away, and no Frenchmen there to fight." He rubbed her back gently, as he'd sometimes done when they were much younger and she'd been distressed about something.

Meg's next words were muffled, sitting as she was with her head on his shoulder. But he heard them clearly enough, for all that.

"Everything would be all right if I had you to help me," she said. "It's a pity I can't marry you."

Meg had said it without thinking, but it felt right. Jon was her best friend—and he'd never teased or pulled her hair like Fred sometimes had. He'd been the one who had backed her up when she wanted to join in their games. The one who'd comforted her when she fell out of a tree, while Fred was busy laughing at her clumsiness. And the one who'd spent hours talking to her when he came home with Fred after Coruña, sharing himself with her while Fred went off drinking with his other friends from childhood.

He had gone very still, his arm stiffening where it still encircled her.

She felt protected, sitting here beside him, his warmth comforting, the feel of his body next to hers reassuring. He would keep her safe.

But he still hadn't spoken. It had been forward of her to suggest it—was he shocked? Offended?

"I'm sorry, Jon. That was—"

"Don't be sorry. Unless you didn't mean it."

Was he agreeing? Oh, she hoped so, but she wished there were more light—she couldn't tell from his voice what he was thinking.

"People will think I'm a jilt." She straightened her spine. "But that's nothing if I escape Rupert."

"They won't believe that of you when they know the circumstances," Jon said, his voice curiously flat. "Shall I ask the vicar to call the banns for us?"

"Will… will he believe you if you say I will not marry Rupert?" He might—he'd known Jon since he was a boy. Then another thought struck and she leaned her head on his shoulder again. "Rupert will say it shows how unfit I am to look after Mama and the farms. And it would be another three weeks—what if he takes Mama? Once he has her… I mean, people will say he's looking after her, and I'm…"

She'd said it all before. Damn Rupert for getting her into this state. And her, for allowing herself to be worn down by him.

"I won't let him take her away. But Meg, I've only got three weeks before I have to return. If you want this, I'll have to get a licence."

"How long will that take?"

"I have to go to Worcester, I think—I'll check with the vicar, or with Mr Trythall. It cannot be above thirty miles, but in this weather… I can't promise to be back by Tuesday morning."

"If I can't find an excuse to delay things, I'll say no at the church." Jon's belief in her gave her heart—she would not let Rupert threaten Mama or herself and get away with it. "If I know you'll be coming back, I don't mind how much fuss it causes or what people say. Rupert cannot do anything in only a day or two."

"That's my girl." He gave her shoulder a quick squeeze and released her.

She felt bereft for a moment, and strangely disappointed at his hearty tone. "Jon, are you sure you're... willing to do this? I... if you are here to back me up, I might—"

"Of course I am." He stood, and pulled her to her feet. "Go in now, Meg; you must be freezing."

No more than he must be—he'd been out in the cold for much longer.

"I'll wait until you've gone in," he added. "The path to the woods is in view of the windows. If anyone sees me leaving, you'll already be safe back in your room."

Not safe. Not yet.

"I'll see you soon, Jon." She stood on tiptoe and kissed his cheek, then slipped out through the door.

Jon watched as Meg trod carefully back across the yard. How much had changed in half an hour! It didn't seem real.

During the last year, he'd spent many an evening in his tent, or in some tumbledown Spanish house where his company had taken shelter, dreaming of coming home to see Meg. Of courting her, in the hope that his feelings might be reciprocated. And dreading that every letter Fred received might bring the news that Meg was betrothed or married.

What he hadn't imagined was being asked to marry

her like this—as a way to save her from her cousin. Was that all she wanted of him? Was he only a safer prospect than Taylor?

He shook his head. He was too tired to think clearly. Another few minutes and Meg should be safely back in her room, then he could set off through the snow again. The morning would be soon enough to go over what had been said here.

CHAPTER 5

Orning came all too soon. The smell of fresh coffee reached Jon before the knock on his door registered, then Becky was picking her way between his discarded garments to set a steaming mug on a small table near the bed.

"What time is it?" he mumbled, as Becky started to pick up stockings and trousers still sodden from the snowdrift he'd fallen into at the edge of the village.

"Nine o'clock. Mr Trythall's here for his breakfast, and asked if you would join him."

Trythall wanted to see him? His clerk must have told him that Jon was back.

"I'll bring up your clean shirt and stockings in a minute," Becky said. "You get that coffee inside you." She tutted as she picked up his trousers. "If you'd hung these up they'd be dryer. Have you got spares?"

"No." He'd replaced his lost shirts and undergarments in Lisbon, but had reserved the rest of his funds for the journey back to England.

"Ah, well. Be sure to sit near the fire in the parlour until you dry out."

"Yes, ma'am!"

Becky left with a laugh.

Trythall was halfway through a plate of ham and eggs when Jon arrived in the parlour. His hair appeared to have receded a little further since Jon saw him last, and his face had put on a little flesh, but he looked up with his usual welcoming expression.

"Glad to see you back safely, Jon," he said, and pointed with his fork to the plate Becky was carrying in. "Eat first; you look like you need it."

Blunt, as usual, but no-one ever took offence. Jon certainly didn't—Trythall had been the one to arrange the sale of the farm after Father had lost more at cards than he could pay. Trythall had done more than that, though— he'd tied up what was left after settling the debts so Father couldn't let that run through his fingers as well.

Jon took the chair indicated, and tucked in with a will. The ham was thick and juicy, the eggs fried to crispy edges but with the yolks still runny, and a second plate held slices of bread and butter to mop up the juices.

He couldn't help comparing it with most of his meals over the last few years, wondering if he'd made the right decision when he joined the army. Mother's sister— married to a rich merchant in Bristol—had helped them to find a house when the farm had been sold, and persuaded her husband to give Father a job. Trythall had offered to train Jon as a clerk—Jon had been grateful, but reluctant, not liking the idea of spending most of his time indoors poring over documents. Trythall had made little protest when Jon expressed a wish to join the army with Fred instead. Money from the farm had purchased his commission, but Jon knew it wouldn't have been possible without Trythall's help.

Jon finally emptied his plate and sat back in the chair, his third mug of coffee in front of him. "Best breakfast I've had in years."

Trythall smiled. "Certainly the best in the last few months, if what I've read in the papers is right. But I'm not here to ask you about that." He tilted his head to one side. "Nor, I imagine, are you in the mood to talk about it."

"No."

"How is your mother?"

"I haven't heard from her for months—her last letter said she was going on well." Father had died early last year. The letter with the news reached Jon at the same time as one written a month later, saying that Mother was settled with her sister. It had seemed pointless to return to England when he'd be too late to be of any use. And the only grief he'd felt was for the years of unhappiness his mother had endured. Father had never lifted a hand against her, but that wasn't the only way a woman's life could be made miserable.

He brought himself back to the present—to his surprise, Trythall was frowning. He hadn't expected censure about that. "I wrote to her from Falmouth, so she knows I am well, and I will go to Bristol before I rejoin my battalion. However, I thought Meg's—Miss Rymer's—situation was more urgent, and it seems I was right."

Trythall's brows rose. "My clerk gave me only the news that you had returned. What's wrong?"

Jon started with Taylor closing the door in his face, and relayed everything Meg had told him, omitting only their proposed solution.

"A sorry tale," Trythall said, when Jon finished. "Now you've mentioned it, I don't remember seeing Miss Rymer or her mother in the village for weeks."

"*Could* Taylor get some kind of legal order to have Mrs Rymer taken away for treatment against the wishes of her daughter? I gathered that Mrs Rymer herself might be too easily influenced."

Trythall shook his head. "That would be most unusual. However, if he did take her without Miss Rymer's blessing, his claim that it would be for Mrs Rymer's own benefit would weigh with many. Miss Rymer could have great difficulty getting her back."

"By which time her mother would have already suffered from those… treatments."

"Indeed. I can see why the situation is worrying. A woman managing alone—it's rarely easy. Your mother had to—" He broke off and shook his head.

"Meg… Miss Rymer thought… That is, I was intending to ask your advice this morning. Miss Rymer only needs to deny her wish to wed Taylor when he brings her to church, but she fears that will only induce him to take things further. She thought… that is, she and I discussed…" Good heavens, why could he not get it out? It wasn't as if he were reluctant to marry her—he only wished it were for a different reason. "She thought being married to someone else would provide the pair of them with protection."

"To you, in particular?"

Jon nodded.

"She does have a point. And I take it you are willing to go through with this—else you would be on your way to Bristol by now?"

"Yes. I wanted to ask what is involved in getting a marriage licence. I need to go to the bishop in Worcester, I think? But I cannot be back before the wedding is set to happen."

"I'm sure I can delay things for a day or two," Trythall said. "If Miss Rymer does not do so herself. You concentrate on getting yourself to Worcester and back."

"Thank you."

"I believe the licence will cost two or three pounds. There is also the matter of a bond for a hundred pounds."

"A *hundred*? I haven't got that much." He had barely ten pounds to his name at the moment.

"You don't need it. The money is forfeit only if you make a false statement about your, and Miss Rymer's, eligibility to marry."

Jon looked down at his shabby jacket with its frayed cuffs, inexpertly mended slash in one sleeve, and stains that would not wash out. "They'll never believe I have enough money for that."

"You have good excuse for your appearance, Jon—they might believe you. But it's of no matter. I will give you a signed and witnessed bond, and also a sealed letter of good character, in case further persuasion is needed."

"Thank you, sir. You're going to a lot of trouble."

"Not much trouble. I dislike seeing women mistreated, and it appears that this is happening to the Rymer ladies at the moment. Your mother…" He glanced out of the window. "Well, never mind that. I'll go and get this bond written for you. Have some more breakfast while you wait. The sky's clear now, but there's no guarantee it will stay that way. It'll be cold, whatever the clouds do. I'll send Becky in, and be back within an hour."

$\sim$

Meg carried Mama's breakfast tray into the kitchen, and paused at the sight of the long, central table covered in mixing bowls, flour jars, and dishes of eggs and butter. Mrs Baines had even unlocked the spice cupboard, and several of the little labelled pots were lined up at one end of the table. But she wasn't measuring or mixing—she was talking to their maid, arms folded across her narrow chest.

"Is something wrong, Mrs Baines?" Meg set the tray down near the edge of the table, pushing a couple of bowls out of the way to make room.

"That's what I'm wondering, Miss. I was going to start baking for a wedding breakfast, but you haven't said how many are coming."

Of course—a wedding was normally an occasion for celebrating.

"I thought I could—" Mrs Baines stopped at the sound of footsteps in the passage, and Morrison strode in.

"Master wants to see Miss Rymer right away." He glanced over the table. "You should be working, not gossiping."

"I'm busy." Meg turned her back on him and began scooping flour into the pan of the weighing scales. The way Morrison had restrained her yesterday had shocked her, but she might be able to take advantage of it. If she didn't meekly obey, would he grasp her arm again in front of Mrs Baines?

"Now, he said." Morrison came closer. At the other end of the room, young Annie was watching with her mouth open, Mrs Baines with narrowed eyes.

"No. This is *my* house, not his." Meg filled the scoop with flour, tempted to fling it into Morrison's face. Morrison grabbed her arm and the scoop flew out of her hand and covered both of them in flour anyway.

"You stupid bit—" He bit off the words as Rupert appeared in the doorway.

"This is your man's fault," she said to Rupert, indicating the flour covering her black gown. "And the second time he has laid hands on me."

If Mrs Baines didn't already know about what had happened yesterday, she did now.

"Cook wanted to know who is coming to the wedding breakfast," Meg went on, before Rupert could reply.

"I thought a celebration would be out of place, my dear, given your recent bereavement." He glanced at the laden table. "I'm sorry to disturb your plans, Mrs Baines. Of course, if you and the others wish to celebrate, by all means bake a cake or two." He smiled at Meg—it almost reached his eyes. "I'm sure, my dear, you may have a couple of friends from the village to join you in our happy occasion. Why don't you come to the parlour with me and let me know who you wish to invite? I can write a note or two, and Morrison can deliver them."

Damn him—he'd made the lack of celebration seem caring. Were Mrs Baines and Annie still convinced he was only concerned for her and Mama?

"Put this stuff away, Annie," Mrs Baines said. "Morrison, get a brush from the cupboard and clear up the mess you've made."

"Clear it up yourself. I've the master's clothes to see to." Morrison stamped out.

"Margaret, my dear?" Rupert said.

Meg sighed and followed him, brushing the flour off her gown as she went.

"I'll bring you tea shortly, Miss Meg," Mrs Baines called after her. "Anything else you want, just call."

Perhaps Rupert hadn't convinced the servants of his sincerity, after all.

Rupert shut the parlour door behind them. Meg felt a moment of unease, but if he were going to force his attentions on her, she thought he would have done it before this. Besides, she could make enough noise for Mrs Baines and Annie to hear, and they wouldn't stand for that happening, no matter how ingratiating Rupert had been.

Had he found out about Jon's return last night?

"I wished to warn you, my dear Margaret, to be ready by nine o'clock tomorrow morning."

Meg let out a silent breath.

"The vicar is not expecting us until eleven, but we don't want to risk the snow delaying our wedding, do we?"

Meg didn't deign to answer.

"Morrison will remain here with your mother. Such a shame she will miss the ceremony, but we wouldn't want to risk her fragile health in the cold."

That threat was clear, then. But could Rupert do anything in the next day or two? The snow would prevent him taking Mama away—but it would also delay Jon's return.

41

Rupert seated himself at the escritoire in one corner of the room. "Now, who do you wish to invite to witness our union?"

"Mr Trythall and Mrs Munnings." Trythall had worked for the Rymers for years, and had been good to Jon.

"Munnings?"

"The landlady of the Swan." A woman who took no nonsense from any man, not even her husband.

Rupert shook his head. "I don't think we want the lower orders present, my dear."

Meg shrugged—a number of curious villagers were likely to attend in any case. "Is that all, cousin?"

She waited until he nodded before leaving; she didn't want to antagonise him unnecessarily.

CHAPTER 6

*J*on nudged the mare sideways at the fingerpost, and reached out to brush the snow from it, unmelted despite the sunny day.

Evesham 1

Still a mile to go, and it would be dark soon. His ride had started under blue skies, heading down from the higher ground of the Cotswolds. Yesterday's fall of snow had filled the lanes, drifting against hedges in impenetrable mounds. He'd had to let the mare pick her way along the edges of the lanes where the stuff was only hock-deep, but still tiring for the poor beast to get through.

It had been almost eleven by the time Jon set out. The landlord had produced a map, and they'd pored over it, concluding that although heading for Evesham first might add a few miles to his journey, from there to Worcester he would be on the turnpike where progress should be quicker. Jon wasn't entirely convinced, as the benefit of the mare not having to push her way through deeper drifts could be countered by previous traffic packing the snow down into uneven ice. But he would be less likely to lose his way on the busier route, and there would be more inns when the mare needed to rest.

Evesham was not half-way to Worcester, though. He hadn't been foolish enough to think he might get there in time to call at the bishop's office today, but he hadn't anticipated that the journey would take quite this long.

"Onwards, girl." He patted the mare's neck, and urged her into motion again. It would be fully dark by the time he reached the town—he would stop to rest the horse and let her eat. It was six or seven miles from Evesham to Pershore along the turnpike road—he should be able to get that far tonight. Possibly a little further, if the thin clouds did not thicken and block the moon.

For now, though, the setting sun painted the clouds in streaks of orange and pink. Smoke rose gently upwards from the farmhouses he passed—intact houses, their timbers not burned for cooking fires by passing armies. Farms with barns full of cows, the animals not slaughtered to feed half-starved soldiers.

This land was home. Perhaps he should stay here.

It was past ten o'clock when Jon rode into the yard of the Angel in Pershore. It seemed no more coaches were expected that night, for only a single lantern provided light in the yard. The moon shone palely through the high cloud, and the surrounding buildings cast impenetrable shadows across the cobbles, but a line of light was visible where the stable doors must be.

Jon dismounted and rubbed the mare's nose. "Some bran mash for you, girl, and a rest." He led her across the yard and knocked on the door. Then knocked again when his first attempt provoked no response.

"What the bloody hell do you want at this hour?" a voice grumbled as the door eased open. The speaker was a silhouette against the light. "It's bad enough with the stagecoaches coming through at all hours. Can't a body get—?"

"Coaches are getting through from Worcester?" Jon asked.

"Said so, didn't I?" A smell of ale and onions wafted out as the man spoke.

A newcomer appeared behind the man. Older, and a little bent, his face in the lantern light showed many lines. "Bugger off back to your ale, Jack, if you're going to be such a grouch." He lifted the lantern to look over the horse before returning his gaze to Jon. "Name's Ben. Come far?" He took the bridle and led the animal across the yard, opening a door that gave onto a row of stalls.

"Other side of Evesham," Jon said. "She needs to eat and drink." Ben grunted and hung the lantern on a hook before stumping off towards the end of the building.

She needed a rub down, too. Jon removed the saddle and picked up a handful of straw, wiping off the sweat so she didn't cool down too fast.

"Look like you've come further than that," Ben said, when he returned with a bucket of water and offered it to the horse. "Back from Spain?"

Jon grunted.

"Had a hard time of it, from what I heard. No need for Jack to be like that."

"I don't mind." Surliness at having to do some work was an improvement on Spanish peasants running off in fear, or desperately trying to protect their remaining food stores from hungry soldiers.

"Must be in a hurry, to travel this late." Ben took the bucket away and patted the mare's neck. "You can have more in a little while, old girl." He turned to Jon. "What's her name? Blackie?"

Number fourteen, the man in Cheltenham had called her. Jon looked at the weary way she stood. He was tired enough, and he'd only been sitting on her.

"Boadicea," he said, on a sudden impulse. She was helping him to eject an invading force.

"Good lass," the groom crooned. "You planning on getting further tonight?"

Jon nodded. "The going's been a little easier since I reached the turnpike. I'd like to get closer to Worcester, if I can."

Ben just stood there, as if waiting for the rest of the story.

"For a marriage licence," Jon added. It was no-one else's business, but Ben was being helpful and friendly.

"Come home to marry your woman, eh? Don't want to waste your leave on banns! She must be a stunner, your woman, to get you out in this weather." He laughed, and it turned into a cough.

"Worth the effort." And that was no exaggeration.

"Get yourself inside, lad," Ben said. "Have something to eat. I'll look after this girl for you for a couple of hours."

As he ate his way through a plate of cold meat and bread by the dying fire in the taproom, all Jon could think of was that Meg was due to marry tomorrow. But even that thought didn't keep him awake for long when they gave him a room and he took off his coat and boots and lay down.

He'd have a couple of hours' sleep—long enough for Boadicea to have a rest—then he'd press on while the moon still shone.

Jon's ability to wake when he wished to had deserted him, and he didn't return to consciousness until a hand shook his shoulder.

"Time to get up, lad."

"Wha…?" He opened his eyes, taking in the glow of a single candle and, on his other side, a faint line of grey between the curtains.

"Damn." He sat up, squinting against the light. "Ben?"

"Ay. I know you wanted to be on your way, but it clouded over—unless you wanted to carry a lantern, you'd not have got far. It's not dawn yet, but there's light enough for you to follow the road. You should be there before noon, if you're lucky."

Oh well, there was no help for it, and Ben might well be right. Jon stood and stretched, reaching for his coat before forcing his feet into his boots.

Out in the stable yard, Ben thrust a mug of over-sweet coffee into his hands, then led a strange horse out from the stables.

"Where's my horse?"

"You want to get home quick, right?" Ben asked.

Jon nodded.

"Take this one, then Boadie'll be fresh when you pick her up on the way back."

JAYNE DAVIS

Boadie? Oh yes—the mare. Jon felt in his pocket for the little pouch of coins that Trythall had given him. He should have enough, and Boadie deserved the rest.

"Pay on the way back," Ben said, taking Jon's empty cup.

"Thank you, Ben."

"Bring her to see me some time. I like to see a pretty woman."

He would—if the plan succeeded. But he couldn't help thinking that if Rupert had his way, Meg might already be married by the time he reached Worcester.

"I'll see you later, Mama." Meg bent to kiss her mother's cheek. "Don't go anywhere, will you? No matter what Rupert or Morrison say."

"No, dear. Of course not." Mama frowned. "Where did you say you were going?"

"I'm going to the village."

"I'll sit with her a while," Mrs Baines said from the doorway. "I've some sewing to do."

Meg straightened. "Thank you." Although Mrs Baines most likely couldn't stop Morrison taking Mama away if he chose to, she'd feel happier if Mama had company.

"He's waiting for you downstairs." Mrs Baines jerked her head towards the door.

Meg grimaced, and went to fetch her coat.

"Just say no, Miss Meg," Mrs Baines whispered as Meg passed her again on her way downstairs.

Meg looked at her, surprised at this unexpected support.

48

"Showed his true colours yesterday," Mrs Baines said quietly, giving Meg a final nod before going to sit next to Mama with her basket of mending.

Meg stood taller as she descended the stairs—it made little practical difference, but somehow knowing she wasn't the only one who didn't trust Rupert made her feel more confident.

Rupert was standing in the hall, one foot tapping impatiently. He turned on his heel when she appeared, and opened the front door. Farlow was waiting outside, with Daisy harnessed to the gig.

Rupert climbed in without waiting for her, and took the reins. Farlow handed her up, and took his place on the backward-facing seat as the gig moved off.

The clear skies of the day before had given way to thick clouds, and the air felt damp. More snow to come, perhaps, although the air had lost its biting chill. As they bumped slowly down the lane, Meg saw that the snow on the bare twigs of the hedges was beginning to melt, but although Daisy still had to plod through a couple of feet of snow, there was not enough of it to prevent them reaching the village. Not reaching the church at all would have been an easier solution—for today—than denying her consent in front of the vicar. At least the melting snow would ease Jon's journey as well.

All too soon they were approaching the final bend before their narrow lane joined the wider road. Meg could see a couple of heads above the hedge—but having to find a gateway to squeeze past someone coming the other way would only take a few minutes.

"Damn!" Rupert's hands went slack on the reins and Daisy stopped.

Meg spirits lifted a little. It wasn't a matter of merely passing the other vehicle, but of getting the gig past a large farm cart with a broken wheel. One, moreover, that appeared to have spilled a load of turnips all over the lane.

Rupert swore again, and scrambled down. As he trudged through the snow, Meg heard exhortations to get that bloody cart moved. She squinted. That was the blacksmith's son, surely, and one of the grooms from the Swan.

Without prompting, Farlow came around to Daisy's head, his shoulders shaking suspiciously.

"Did you know about this, Farlow?"

"No, Miss." He grinned. "Looks like you've got more friends than you thought." He looked over his shoulder. "I'll go and give them a hand with those turnips."

Rupert was waving his arms at the blacksmith's son while Farlow joined the groom, who appeared to be doing little more than spreading the turnips more evenly across the snow. Meg sighed—although she was grateful for the delay, this lane wasn't the only way into Upper Westley. There was still plenty of time to take the longer way around.

CHAPTER 7

*J*on finally spotted the tower of Worcester Cathedral late in the morning. He'd been to the city once or twice in his youth, and recalled stopping at the King's Head, on the road in. When he reached it, he rode under the arch into the stable yard. A few coins changed hands, and an ostler led the horse away to be watered, fed, and rested. Jon went into the taproom for directions and something to eat.

"Bishop?" the barmaid said. "Lives out at Hartlebury most of the time. That's a few miles on the Kidderminster Road."

Hartlebury?

"Here, sit down, love."

She pushed him towards a table near the fire, and he sank onto the bench, resting his head against the wall behind. *Another few miles?*

The barmaid returned with a pint of ale and set it on the table, then drew up a chair and sat, leaning forward

JAYNE DAVIS

on her elbows. Jon took a long pull at his ale. She was a plump lass, with a face that looked as if she laughed a lot.

"You look a right mess, love. The bishop might be at the Palace here, but is it him you want, or his office?"

He could see only friendly concern in her expression, and his business wasn't a secret. Telling Ben in Pershore had done no harm—had helped, in fact. "Marriage licence," he said. "Don't want to waste my leave."

"Ah!" A beaming smile spread across her face. "It's the bishop's *office* you want. We get a few in here wanting one of them."

Thank God. A few miles less now was also less for the return journey.

"You want some food? You might have to wait a bit—it won't do to expire in the waiting room." She sniggered. "That'd put the cat amongst the pigeons right enough, with that stuffy lot."

Jon nodded, and she bustled off. She was accosted by other customers, but before too long a thin man enveloped in a huge apron brought a bowl of green soup, with hunks of fresh bread and a dish of butter. Pea soup had never been his favourite, but it was hot and he wolfed it down, accepting a slice of beef pie to follow when it was offered.

The bishop's office wasn't far, but the barmaid was right—he had to wait. The ante-room had only a meagre fire burning in the grate, but it was dry and he'd slept in worse places. He leaned back in the chair, stretching his legs out before him. If he did fall asleep, they'd surely wake him when it was his turn, if only to get his scruffy person and muddy boots out of the way.

~

Meg heard the church clock striking as the gig approached the first houses in the village. It was half an hour after the time arranged for their wedding, and also only half an hour before noon, when it would be too late to hold a wedding that day.

Would the vicar still be there?

It had taken some time to turn the gig in the lane, and Rupert's temper had been tested further by finding even deeper snow on the longer route, which made poor Daisy go more slowly still. Then they'd come across a herd of cows ambling along the road, accompanied by an uncommunicative yokel who refused to be hurried or divert them into a field to let the gig pass.

Meg didn't recognise the cows—who, apart from their owner, would? But she did recognise the man with them as the cowman of one of her tenants, and carefully avoided meeting his eyes. The cows should have been safe in their barn for the last couple of months, not being herded along snowy lanes, but Rupert wouldn't know that.

And now they were in Upper Westley, and Rupert's lips compressed as he saw the church doors closed.

"Go and see if anyone's there, Farlow," he ordered.

Farlow went through the lych gate and into the porch. He reappeared only a few moments later, another man beside him. Not a gentleman, by his clothing, Meg thought, although it was difficult to tell when everyone was muffled up in scarves and warm hats.

"Door's locked," Farlow announced when he returned.

"This chap wants a word. Shall I see if Vicar's at home while he talks to you?"

"No. Get up behind," Rupert snapped, and flicked the reins to set Daisy into motion, leaving the unknown man staring after them.

The vicarage was only a few yards down the lane. "Wait here," Rupert commanded as he pulled up outside the gate and descended. He stalked up the path and banged on the door; the vicar's housekeeper opened it and Rupert was admitted. As they watched, the stranger skirted the gig and went to wait beside the vicarage door.

Meg wasn't sure whether to be relieved or dismayed when the door reopened and Rupert came out alone. She wanted to speak to the vicar, to explain her situation, but not with Rupert present. If she couldn't avoid Rupert, it was better to explain herself in church with other witnesses present—it did seem that at least some of the villagers would take her side.

Rupert and the stranger had a brief conversation in the vicarage garden before her cousin returned to the gig, his expression furious. They drove back to Oakdene in silence, the turnips and broken cart no longer in evidence.

Reprieve for another day—and Jon should be back tomorrow.

Boadicea carried Jon out of Evesham again in the grey dawn light, his surroundings becoming more familiar as the rising slopes ahead indicted the approaching end to their journey. Although he'd succeeded in his mission— the licence was safely stowed in an inner pocket—he didn't dare hope that he would actually be marrying Meg. Not until he learned whether or not he was too late.

No, Meg would refuse to marry Taylor.

She *must*.

The rain didn't help. It was beginning to melt the snow, but it soaked into his coat and trousers, and trickles ran down inside his collar when a gust blew in the wrong direction. The landscape was as bleak as the Spanish high plains, and he tried to imagine how it would look later in the year.

In a few months, these hedgerows would be sprinkled with green buds of hawthorn, white blackthorn flowers, and primroses in the banks. Cows would be grazing in the meadows beyond, and corn growing in the fields. Then, later, the summer sun would provide comfortable warmth, not the baking heat of a Spanish summer.

Somewhere across the fields, a church clock began to strike the hour. He didn't count the strokes—he would be in the village as soon as Boadie could carry him there, and Meg would already be married or she would not. Knowing the hour would not help.

He cursed himself again for taking the wrong road out of Evesham in the dark—he'd lost several hours by the time he'd realised his mistake and backtracked. But now the fingerposts had Upper Westley on them—only a few miles to go.

Meg hunched inside her coat as Rupert drove the gig into the village. There'd been no turnips this morning, no cows or even sheep. But Rupert had insisted they set off at eight o'clock, so they might have passed by too early for further attempts at delay. It was probably just as well. Rupert had been in a foul mood for the rest of yesterday, renewing his threats to her mother if she failed to marry him the next day.

Today, now.

And today Morrison was riding on the seat behind them, not Farlow. Rupert must have realised there was little any of the servants could to do to spirit Mama to safety without the gig.

When they came to a stop outside the church, Rupert ordered her down and took her arm to pull her towards the door. Morrison led Daisy and the gig on—towards the Swan, Meg hoped. There was no need for the animal to stand around in the cold and wet, even if Rupert seemed to be eschewing the warmth of a parlour at the inn.

The inner door of the church was locked, as it had been yesterday. Rupert sat on one of the stone benches that lined the sides of the porch, but Meg was cold from sitting still in the gig and paced up and down the small space.

After ten minutes or so the sexton appeared, brandishing a key. "Vicar's finishing his breakfast," he said as he unlocked the door. "He'll be along in half an hour or so."

"Thank you." Rupert looked as if he'd had to force the words out.

Cold seemed to radiate from the church walls as Rupert pushed her to sit in one of the front pews, but Meg didn't mind. She felt safer here than she would locked in a private parlour with him.

She felt even safer ten minutes later. The sound of the

door latch echoed in the still air, and Rupert sprang up with an eager look on his face. His change of expression when he saw that it wasn't the vicar but Mrs Munnings would have been comical, had her nerves not been tying her stomach in knots.

"You can't come in here," Rupert protested. "This is a private—"

"No such thing as a private wedding in this village," Mrs Munnings asserted, folding her arms. "You going to assault me in God's house?" she added as Rupert moved towards her.

Rupert took a deep breath and returned to his seat, a muscle in his jaw working. He made no further move, keeping his eyes on the stained glass window above the altar as the blacksmith and his son appeared, along with the barmaid from the Swan, the grocer, the stranger from the day before, and the attorney.

Mr Trythall nodded at her as he sat down in the front pew across the aisle, and some of Meg's tension relaxed. He'd always been a good friend to her family—more so to Jon. Was he behind all this? She sensed that these people were on her side.

Then the vicar arrived, brushing drops of rain from the shoulders of his black cassock. He was a tall, stout man, his hair sprinkled with grey. He stopped beside their pew. "Miss Rymer, would you accompany me into the vestry, if you please?"

Meg stood, but Rupert did too, and placed her hand on his elbow as they followed the vicar.

"Is this really necessary?" Rupert asked as the vicar closed the vestry door behind them. "My dear Margaret has enough to put up with nursing her ailing mother, particularly after yesterday's unfortunate delays. We *did* arrive before noon yesterday, so our marriage then would have been perfectly legal."

The vicar removed his spectacles and began to polish them on a handkerchief. "That would not have allowed time for this little talk before the ceremony, Mr Taylor. I thought I made that clear yesterday."

"You did, sir. I'm sorry for my impatience."

Meg almost winced at the overdone penitence in Rupert's manner.

The vicar's brows rose. "Very good. As you know, marriage is a holy state ordained by God, and not to be taken lightly. Or…" He replaced his spectacles and focussed on Rupert. "Or to be undertaken without the full and free consent of both parties." He turned to Meg. "Do you freely consent to this marriage, Miss Rymer?"

Meg drew a deep breath. "No, I do not."

"My dear!" Rupert moved to take her hand, but she wrenched it from his grip.

"Mr Taylor has prevented me from coming into the village to let you know, and he has threatened to have my mother taken to an asylum."

"Is this true, Mr Taylor?"

Rupert gave a deprecating laugh. "I would argue with the phrasing, sir. My dear Margaret refuses to admit that her poor Mama is becoming worse. Mrs Rymer is my blood relative, my father's dear sister, and if Margaret will not follow my physician's advice, it behoves me to do so."

The vicar nodded, and Meg's heart sank. She would still refuse to say the words, but it would be so much easier if the vicar supported her.

"How is this relevant to the subject of Miss Rymer's

consent?" the vicar asked. "The two matters appear unrelated."

"Only that Margaret herself is confused, sir."

"Indeed?"

"I am not!"

"Don't worry, my dear," the vicar said. "Mr Taylor's statement is sufficient. I will—" He broke off as a babble of voices sounded beyond the door.

CHAPTER 8

*T*he first thing Jon saw when he rode into Upper Westley was Charlie Allsup, the grocer's son, waiting at the turning for the church, seemingly oblivious to the rain. Charlie beckoned, and Jon kicked Boadie into a canter.

"They're in the church! Hurry!"

Jon turned down the lane and dismounted outside the lych gate. He threw the reins over Boadie's head, leaving her to crop grass in the verge.

Heads of a dozen people inside the church turned as he pushed the door open. They were all in the pews— there was no-one standing before the altar.

Were they signing the register? Was he too late after all?

Then a babble of voices rose, and he saw Trythall walking towards him. The smile on his friend's face turned Jon limp with relief, and he grabbed the end of the back pew to stop himself falling.

"You've got it?" Trythall asked.

Jon nodded.

"Well done, lad! Things'll be easier with you back. Vicar's taken them into…"

Jon didn't hear the rest of Trythall's words, for the vestry door opened and the vicar came out. Behind him stood Meg, with Rupert's hand gripping one arm.

"Jon!"

She was beautiful to him, in spite of the black gown draining the colour from her skin and the anxiety on her face. An anxiety that did not dissipate now he had arrived.

"What are you doing here?" Rupert released Meg and stepped forward. "This is none of your business!"

The villagers turned their attention from Rupert back to Jon.

"I've come to marry Meg."

A ragged cheer broke out.

"Silence!" The vicar's voice thundered between the stone walls. "This is the house of God, and I will not have it made into a side show!"

"Sit down, lad, before you fall down." Trythall's voice was quiet, and he pulled Jon to sit beside him in the back pew.

The vicar glared at the congregation until the chatter died away and everyone resumed their seats. Then he turned to Meg. "Miss Rymer, do you consent to marry Mr Taylor?"

"I do not." Her voice was clear and firm.

She *wasn't* married. Trythall had implied as much, but now he believed it.

"Mr Taylor, you suggested that Miss Rymer is confused. Do you still maintain that?"

61

A murmur arose in the congregation but ceased at another glare from the vicar.

"She will not send her mother—"

"Yes or no?"

"I… er…" Rupert glanced around.

"I shall save you the bother." The vicar drew himself up to his full height. "Either Miss Rymer is in her right mind, in which case she refuses to marry you. Or she is mentally confused, in which case she is not *capable* of giving consent. In addition, you lied when you told me that Miss Rymer consented to the banns being called. Leave this church now!"

"Good man," Trythall said, low-voiced.

But Rupert still stood near the altar rail, now staring at the back of the church.

"What are you waiting for?" the vicar asked impatiently.

"Who's that?" Jon asked. A stranger was walking down the aisle, to whispers from the watching villagers.

"Don't know him," Trythall said, "but he's been hanging around the village for the last couple of days."

The man bowed to the vicar. He didn't raise his voice, but his words still carried clearly in the waiting silence.

"I apologise, sir, for raising this matter in a church, but I have a warrant for this man's arrest, for debt. A debt that he promised would be paid instantly in the event of his marriage."

"You two." The vicar pointed at two of the village men. "Escort Taylor from the church. What happens to him after that is none of my business. The rest of you may go as well. There will be no wedding here today. If you wish to discuss the matter, you may do so in the Swan."

Jon rested his head against the pew in front of him. Meg hadn't needed his help in the end. And with Rupert arrested, her cousin was no longer a threat to her or her mother.

She didn't need him, either.

He was back! Meg took in the water pooling on the floor at Jon's feet and the lines of fatigue around his eyes, visible even from this distance, and suddenly her flash of joy vanished. His face looked thinner than she remembered, too—this was the first time in a year that she'd seen him in daylight.

Rupert's grip on her arm tightened, then he swore under his breath before he headed towards Jon. Meg turned her attention to the vicar, managing a firm denial that she consented to marry her cousin. Then Rupert was escorted from the church and it seemed her problems were over. Mrs Munnings and Becky came to say how glad they were that things had turned out all right, and she managed to thank the blacksmith and the cowman for their efforts the day before.

But all she could think about was the weather Jon had endured on his trip to Worcester and back, all because she hadn't believed that saying no in church would be enough. And when the vicar dispersed the small crowd around her, Jon was no longer at the back of the church. She went out into the porch, but he was nowhere in sight.

Morrison—where was he?

"Miss Rymer!" Mr Trythall stood beside her, with a twinkle in his eye.

"I am sorry—did I ignore you?"

"You did, but understandably. Will you allow me to drive you home?" He opened a large umbrella. "Your gig is at the Swan."

"Is Morrison there?" If he was, he could not be threatening Mama.

"I advised the constable to lock him up until he can be questioned about his involvement."

That was one worry out of the way for now. She took his offered arm, and they set off.

"You will want to get back to your mama, I think?" Mr Trythall went on.

"Yes. I mean, no! Where is J— Lieutenant Lewis?"

"Mrs Munnings has taken him away to be dried off, warmed up, and fed."

"All that way, and for nothing…" He'd done it for her, willingly. She knew then that what she felt for him wasn't merely friendship, it was love. She didn't want to leave the village without thanking him, at the very least. "Thank you for your kind offer, sir, but I can drive the gig myself."

"Good heavens, not in this weather, and with snow still in the lanes! I will ride behind if you prefer to drive yourself. And I will be able to report back to Jon that you are home and safe."

"I must see him first, to…" To say that although her proposal to him had been made to help her escape, she *wanted* him in her life.

"If you wish, my dear, but pray do consider—your mama will be worried, and Jon… Well, I think you should both rest and put this nasty business with your cousin out of your minds before you talk. Now, here is the gig ready for you—do I ask for your horse to be unharnessed?"

Meg hesitated as Mr Trythall patiently held the

umbrella over her. What he said made sense, although it seemed wrong to just leave.

"You will pass on my thanks to Jon, will you not, sir?"

"Indeed, I will. When I return." He shouted for his own horse, and had it tied to the gig, then handed Meg up. "If you hold the umbrella, my dear, we may both stay reasonably dry."

Meg looked back over her shoulder at the Swan, watching it grow smaller as Daisy plodded along, then turned her gaze resolutely ahead. If she knew Mrs Munnings, Jon would be in a hot bath now; then—if he had any sense—in bed. And she could always drive herself back into the village once she was sure Mama was all right.

Yesterday's delays—someone must have organised that. "Sir, do I have you to thank for the turnips and cows?"

"I did suggest to various people that a delay in the proceedings might be helpful."

Strange, she had never seen a twinkle in his eyes before—but then she had only had business with him after her father died, and when they heard that Fred had been killed.

"You said, Miss Rymer, that Jon had ridden to Worcester for nothing, but I do not agree. If not for your cousin's arrest, he might still have made life difficult for you, and none of us knew that would happen." He glanced at her. "If nothing else, the licence he has would have been an insurance policy."

What did Jon think—did he *want* to marry her or—?

No. She would not think of that now.

"You have been very good to me, Mr Trythall, but you hardly know me."

"To be frank, I did it for Jon as much as for you." Trythall's face reddened. "If… if things had gone differently… well, in short, at one time I courted his mother, but…" He sighed. "I sometimes think of him as the son I never had." He looked at her. "That is not to say I would not have done it all anyway—I do not like coercion and manipulation, not to mention lying to a man of God."

"I do thank you, sir, whatever your motivation."

"Yes, well…" He reddened again, but she thought she detected a pleased smile.

Jon pushed his plate away, shaking his head as Becky offered him more. He hadn't felt like eating, but knew he should have something before setting off for Oakdene. There would be time enough for food once his future was decided.

He'd refused the bath Mrs Munnings had suggested—a wash in front of a roaring fire had warmed him sufficiently before he donned one of Sam Munnings' shirts and a borrowed neckcloth. Mrs Munnings had done her best with the mud on his trousers, and someone had rinsed his boots for him. It didn't matter—he'd get wet again on the way. Meg deserved to be courted by someone clean, bearing flowers or other gifts, but hc couldn't manage that.

"You want your horse?" Becky asked.

"She's called Boadicea," Jon said, while he considered. It was only a few miles, and the going this morning hadn't been too hard on the mare. There wasn't a spare stall in the stable at Oakdene, but there would be enough room for her to shelter for a while. "I'll go and saddle her myself."

"Good luck, love." Becky gave him a swift peck on the cheek before heading back to the kitchens.

Jon gaped after her for a moment, but he shouldn't have been surprised. He had announced his wish to wed Meg in the church, and any villagers not there would have heard by now.

He headed for the stables, where the mare eyed him with an air of weary resignation. The poor animal must be used to being taken out in all weathers, and probably ridden as hard as he had used her. As he mounted up and clattered out of the yard, he wondered how much it would cost to buy her from the coaching inn in Cheltenham, then shook his head. He needed to decide his own future first. Or at least, he needed Meg to decide his future.

When he came to the road junction with the fingerpost he stopped, as he had… was it really only three days ago? The woods were blacker now, melting snow revealing wet bark on trunks and twigs. Some impulse made him dismount and lead Boadie along the path, past places he remembered playing, and the overgrown side routes off to the best trees for climbing or the clearings where the sun shone in spring. Soon there would be snowdrops beneath the trees, then primroses and sweet violets, celandines, and wood anemones. As he walked, some of his thoughts from the journey to Worcester coalesced in his mind and he came to a decision. He was not going to Jersey to spend his days training up recalcitrant recruits, and watching boys still wet behind the ears promoted above him because their parents had money or influence.

No—whether or not Meg wanted him, he would sell his commission.

CHAPTER 9

Farlow, Mrs Baines, and Annie came running as Trythall pulled the gig to a stop outside the front door.

"Oh, Miss, you did give us a turn when we saw you being driven back!" Mrs Baines gasped.

"Not to worry, my dear," Trythall said, before Meg could speak. "Mr Taylor has been apprehended by the law for debt, and will bother Miss Rymer no more." He descended from the gig.

"Good news, Miss Rymer," Farlow said, more sedately. "Are you staying, Mr Trythall?"

"Do come in for some refreshment," Meg said.

"No, no, I must get back." He unhitched his horse as he spoke, and mounted it. "I will give your message to Lieutenant Lewis, Miss Rymer." He cantered off down the drive, and Meg turned to go into the house, leaving Farlow to unhitch Daisy.

"Make some tea, if you please, Mrs Baines," Meg said, removing her wet pelisse and handing it to Annie.

"Miss…" Mrs Baines remained where she was, hands clutched in front of her. "Miss, I'm sorry if I took Mr Taylor's part at any time. We didn't—"

"Don't worry, Mrs Baines—he was very plausible." So much so that he'd made her doubt herself—she could hardly blame the servants. "Is Mama upstairs?"

"Yes, Miss."

Mrs Baines hurried off, and Meg went upstairs. Mama sat by the window, knitting.

"Who was that with you?" she asked. "Is he back?"

"Mr Trythall drove me home," Meg said, not even trying to work out who Mama meant by 'he'. "Cousin Rupert has… has gone, and won't be back." There was little point in explaining further.

"Oh, good. I know you didn't like him, dear. Did you have a nice time in the village?"

Meg was saved from replying by the arrival of tea and a plate of biscuits. It was only as she sank into a chair and took a mouthful of tea that she realised how tired she was. She could relax now—all her troubles were over.

Apart from Jon. Not that he was a trouble, but he'd agreed to marry her because she asked him, and had convinced him she needed his help. But did he *want* to be with her the way she wanted to be with him?

"Oh, we have another caller," Mama said. "Someone is riding along the lane."

Jon was here already? Meg rushed to the window, but the rider was already out of sight.

She swallowed the rest of her tea, almost burning her throat, and hurried to her own room. A quick pull of a comb through her hair sorted out some of the tangles, and she swiftly pinned it into a simple knot. She could do nothing about the shadows under her eyes, or the drab mourning gown, but she smoothed her skirts as she descended the stairs.

Farlow had already answered the door. "A Mr Dutton to see you, Miss."

The Rymers' stable should have been a welcome sight as Jon emerged from the woods. Boadie, at least, would be comfortable for a while, even if there wasn't much space for three horses inside. But Jon felt as tense as he did before a battle; the next hour could decide his future happiness.

There were two strange horses outside the stable, both saddled. And Meg stood just inside the open door, talking to the bailiff who'd been at the church. Were Rupert's debts *still* causing her problems?

He dropped Boadie's reins and hurried towards them. "Meg, is everything all right?"

The smile she turned on him scattered his thoughts for a moment.

"Dutton." The bailiff held out a hand and Jon shook it automatically. "I've come for any of Mr Taylor's possessions that are here."

"Mr Trythall drove me back, Jon, and Mr Dutton met him on the road. He said there was no problem in releasing Rupert's things."

"He was so good as to provide me with a note to that effect," Dutton said.

Jon glanced at the proffered paper, torn from a notebook by the looks of it. As before, Meg hadn't needed his help.

"I'll be on my way, then, Miss. Someone will collect the trunk in a day or two." Dutton nodded to Jon and mounted one of the horses, leading the other away.

"Trunk?"

Meg smiled, although not the happy smile she'd greeted him with. "I left Farlow throwing—and I use the word deliberately—Rupert's belongings into the trunk he arrived with. There'll soon be no trace of him in the house."

"That's good."

"Jon, come in out of the rain. Now Dutton has taken Rupert's horse away, there's plenty of room for yours."

"This is Boadicea," Jon said as he followed her into the dim shelter of the stable. "She's worked hard for the last few days." Why was he babbling about the horse?

"Some oats for you, then, once we've dried you off." Meg rubbed the mare's nose. "Unsaddle her, Jon."

Meg went off to the end of the stable, returning with a bucket of water and two brushes. She handed one to Jon, and they stood on opposite sides of Boadie, brushing her down.

He took a deep breath. "Meg, I know you only asked me—"

"Jon, when I asked you—" Meg said at the same time.

There was an awkward silence.

"Meg, I didn't agree—"

"Jon, it wasn't—"

This time he met her eyes as they both stopped talking, and her face lit with the mischievous grin he remembered from their childhood. No—there was more than that in her eyes.

Much more.

It took only a moment for him to move around the horse and take her in his arms. The way she clung to him before turning her face up towards his said more than words ever could.

"Kiss me," she whispered, and his last shred of doubt vanished.

He bent his head towards hers and his fingers tangled in her hair. His tiredness seemed to drain away as her lips parted beneath his and she responded with all the enthusiasm he could have wished for.

Mrs Baines had only needed a look at Meg's face when she and Jon returned from the stable to see that celebrations were in order. By the time Meg came back to the kitchen after giving Mama the news, the cook was getting out flour, butter, and eggs, muttering something about Mr Jon needing to be fattened up. Meg hid her smile, and put the kettle on the range herself. She'd only had a few mouthfuls of tea before Mr Dutton called, and she hadn't managed to eat anything for breakfast this morning. She set out plates of biscuits and cake, and some slices of cold pigeon pie that Mrs Baines had in the larder.

This morning—such a short time for everything to have changed.

She carried the tray into the parlour. Mama was now installed in her proper place beside the fire, although she was still knitting. Jon…

Jon was sprawled in a chair, stockinged feet warming by the fire, asleep. Relaxed, his face looked years younger than it had in church this morning, and she felt a lump in her throat. That licence would not be wasted after all—they had only a few weeks before he had to return.

She set the tray down quietly, not wanting to wake him, but when she looked up again his eyes were open.

"Sorry." He looked so much like a boy about to be chastised that Meg laughed.

"Don't be silly, dear," Mama said. "There's nothing like a little nap when you're tired." She put her knitting to one side. "I said everything would be all right when he came back, didn't I?"

"You were right, Mama."

"When is the wedding?"

"As soon as the vicar will do it…" Meg paused—she should consider more than her own wishes. "No. Jon—your Mama will wish to come, will she not? You will have to go and see her. But how long do you have?"

Jon leaned forward, elbows resting on his knees. "I'm going to sell out, Meg. That is, if you have no objection to a husband with little knowledge about managing farms but a great desire to learn. Father would never teach me anything about it."

"Only if that husband is you, Jon." She wanted him to hold her close again, but Mama's presence prevented that. "Shall we call the banns? That will give you time to fetch your mother from Bristol, and we can marry in the middle of January." There was enough room here for Mrs Lewis to stay permanently, if she wanted to—at least, until babies arrived. Meg felt heat rising to her cheeks at the thought, and hurried on. "I suppose you will have to go to London to sell your commission."

"Yes. I need to get some new clothes, too. But three weeks gives me time enough for that."

She would gladly take him as he was, but he was eyeing the slices of pie, so she didn't say so. They could discuss all the details later. For now she would enjoy the anticipation, and assist Mrs Baines in feeding him up.

"Have some pigeon pie, Jon."

May 1813

Jon checked the harnesses on Daisy and Boadie. They made an odd couple—the shiny landau he had borrowed from the magistrate should rightly be drawn by a matched pair, but these two animals were almost family. Meg had woven ribbons into their manes, and they made a pretty sight in the spring sunshine. It was very different from the gentle snow that had fallen when he married Meg four months ago, but the weather then had not mattered to them.

Meg came out of the house, lifting her skirts to keep them well away from the dust in the cobbled yard. She'd bought a new gown for the occasion, but she was beautiful whatever she wore. Their mothers followed her out, also in new gowns.

He handed them into the landau and climbed in, and Farlow flicked the reins to set the horses in motion. Sitting beside Meg on the rear-facing seat, Jon watched the countryside unrolling behind them. The hedgerows in leaf and flower, bluebells colouring the woodland beneath the budding trees—all as he had imagined on that wet ride back from Worcester. He'd got one thing wrong though— this place was home, not for the countryside, but because he was with Meg. He reached for her hand, feeling the answering pressure of her fingers on his.

The whole village seemed to have turned out for the wedding. Meg and Mrs Rymer went in first, and Jon offered his arm to his mother. They walked together from the sunshine into the cool of the church, where Mr Trythall awaited them with an eager smile. Mother, too, would now have a loving husband.

Jon looked at Meg as the vicar read the opening words of the ceremony, and she met his eyes with the smile that still filled him with joy. If his mother and Mr Trythall could be even half as happy as he and Meg were, all would be well.

Thank you for reading *Saving Meg*; I hope you enjoyed it. If you can spare a few minutes, I'd be very grateful if you could review this book on Amazon or Goodreads.

The story was inspired by Robert Frost's poem "Stopping by Woods on a Snowy Evening"—mainly the idea of the snow, and a man who has promises to keep.

Find out about my other books on the following pages or on my website.

www.jaynedavisromance.co.uk

If you want news of special offers or new releases, join my mailing list via the red box on the contact page on my website. I won't bombard you with emails, I promise!

Alternatively, follow me on Facebook - links are on my website.

ABOUT THE AUTHOR

I wanted to be a writer when I was in my teens, hooked on Jane Austen and Georgette Heyer (and lots of other authors). Real life intervened, and I had several careers, including as a non-fiction author under another name. That wasn't *quite* the writing career I had in mind!

Now I am lucky enough to be able to spend most of my time writing, when I'm not out walking, cycling, or enjoying my garden.

THE MARSTONE SERIES

A duelling viscount, a courageous poor relation and an overbearing lord—just a few of the characters you will meet in The Marstone Series. From windswept Devonshire, to Georgian London and revolutionary France, true love is always on the horizon and shady dealings often afoot.

The series is named after Will, who becomes the 9th Earl of Marstone. He appears in all the stories, although often in a minor role.

Each book can be read as a standalone story, but readers of the series will enjoy meeting characters from previous books.

They are all available on Kindle (including Kindle Unlimited) and in paperback.

SAUCE FOR THE GANDER - BOOK 1

A duel. An ultimatum. An arranged marriage.

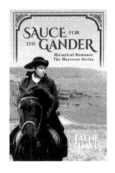

England, 1777

Will, Viscount Wingrave, whiles away his time gambling and bedding married women, thwarted in his wish to serve his country by his controlling father. News that his errant son has fought a duel with a jealous husband is the last straw for the Earl of Marstone. He decrees that Will must marry. The earl's eye lights upon Connie Charters, daughter of a poor but socially ambitious father.

Connie wants a husband who will love and respect her, not a womaniser and a gambler. When her conniving father forces the match, she has no choice but to agree.

Will and Connie meet for the first time at the altar. As they settle into their new home on the wild coast of Devonshire, the young couple find they have more in common than they thought. But there are dangerous secrets that threaten both them and the nation.

Can Will and Connie overcome the dark forces that conspire against them and find happiness together?

Other books in the Marstone Series

Standalone stories

Lightning Source UK Ltd.
Milton Keynes UK
UKHW021540040122
396600UK00011B/2896